For Elora and Iona,
daughters of a dreamer.

W(OF)OLF WESSEX

MATTHEW HARFFY

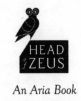

HEAD
ZEUS

An Aria Book

WOLF OF WESSEX

BY MATTHEW HARFFY

The Bernicia Chronicles

The Serpent Sword
The Cross and the Curse
Blood and Blade
Killer of Kings
Warrior of Woden
Storm of Steel
Fortress of Fury
Kin of Cain (short story)

Wolf of Wessex